The Little Red Hen

illustrated
by
STEPHEN HOLMES

based on a traditional folk tale

Once upon a time ther
red hen who lived on a

One morning, the little r
some grains of wheat. She
to her friends in the farmyai

"Who will help me to plant this wheat?" the little red hen asked her friends.

"Not I," said the cat.

"Not I," said the rat.

"Not I," said the pig.

"Then I shall plant the wheat myself," said the little red hen.

And that's just what she did. She planted the grains in a neat row in the sunniest part of the field.

The little red hen looked after the wheat carefully. She watered it and watched it grow.

At last the wheat was tall and strong and golden. The little red hen knew it was ready to be cut.

"Who will help me to cut the wheat?"
the little red hen asked her friends.

"Not I," said the cat.

"Not I," said the rat.

"Not I," said the pig.

"Then I shall cut the wheat myself,"
said the little red hen.

And that's just what she did. With her
little scythe, she carefully cut down
each stalk of golden wheat.

Then she went back to her friends.
"Who will help me to take
the wheat to the miller?"
she asked.

"Not I," said the cat.

"Not I," said the rat.

"Not I," said the pig.

"Then I shall take the wheat to the miller myself," said the little red hen.

And that's just what she did. She carried the wheat to the mill, and the miller ground it into flour. He put the flour into a sack for the little red hen.

The little red hen took the sack of flour back to the farmyard.

"Who will help me to take this flour to the baker?" she asked her friends.

"Not I," said the cat.

"Not I," said the rat.

"Not I," said the pig.

"Then I shall take it to the baker myself," said the little red hen.

And that's just what she did. The baker made the flour into a loaf of fresh, tasty bread. The little red hen took it back to the farmyard.

"Who will help me to eat this bread?" the little red hen asked her friends.

"I will!" said the cat.

"I will!" said the rat.

"I will!" said the pig.

"No, you will not!" said the little red hen. "I shall eat this fresh, tasty bread all by myself!"

And that's just what she did!